survival

Daniel Powell

DISTILLATIONS PRESS
JACKSONVILLE, FLORIDA

PUBLISHED BY DISTILLATIONS PRESS
JACKSONVILLE, FLORIDA

BOOK DESIGN BY CANOPY STUDIOS

ISBN-13: 978-0615496252 (Distillations Press)
ISBN-10: 0615496253

Printed in the United States of America

Jacksonville, Florida and Charleston, South Carolina

survival

The man and his son braced themselves against the cold, huddled there on the park bench, their breath punctuated by little blasts of steam. The boy made fists tight as frozen potatoes, clenching and unclenching his hands as his father drilled the words into him.

"Ok, you've made it this far, Son. You remember that when things get hairy in there. I don't have to tell you how many folks never even make it to Labor, do I? But your old man made it, and you will too. I'm sure of it. Ok, kid, what's the first rule?"

"Look for cover."

"Damn straight. You kill time that way. Killing time is the name of this here game. Rule two?"

"Cover ground by night."

"Good. That's right, Son. You wait for dusk and get a lead on those bastards. Don't let 'em lull you into complacency. It's an old trick. When the sun goes down, *you* get moving. Rule three?"

The boy looked into his father's eyes, a pair of ruddy brown pools, the whites streaked though with crimson veins. Sleep had been fleeting for all of them in the weeks since the baby's due date fell into testing range. He swallowed hard.

"A kill is as good as a victory," he replied, the words barely above a whisper.

His father nodded. He stared at his son, tears welling in his eyes. He reached across the bench and pulled him into an embrace, the young man's thin shoulder blades sharp as pottery shards beneath his windbreaker. "I know it's tough, Bryan. God, but I know it, Son. But you do what you have to do, you understand? They'll *kill* you in there. You do what you have to do to ensure *your survival*," he said.

The boy flinched. His father had called him by his given name—a rarity indeed. The sudden intimacy kicked his pulse up another notch. Jesus, this was happening.

"You ready?" the old man said.

The boy's name was Bryan Norton. He was tall and thin, still awkward in his youth, with cords of muscle and quick, nervous blue eyes. If he survived the world on the other side of the iron wall, he would emerge from the test a man.

And he would be a father.

"I think so, Pop. Tell Mom that I love her. Tell her I'd like some of her lasagna tomorrow night for supper." He choked on a sob. "And tell Maggie that I'll be there, Dad. Tell her...tell her that I promise," his voice cracked, "that I'll be there."

A tear tracked down the old man's face as he regarded his only son. He opened his mouth but his words were swallowed by the din of the air-raid siren. Labor had officially begun. All around them, men in blue jeans, long-sleeved thermal tops and white wind breakers began to walk toward the processing stations, their left hands extended for fingerprint verification.

Grief reigned on the periphery of the processing area. Parents and siblings wailed as they watched their loved ones disappear into the stalls where they would be processed before entering the Labor field.

In Portland, the survival rate for men entering Labor hovered around 60%, far better than in many places. A general belief held that America's western cities had kinder bulls—that places like Seattle, Portland and San Francisco were easier to survive than the Labor fields in Pittsburgh or Detroit.

Bryan spared a single glance over his shoulder at his father, his old man a haggard shadow of his usual gregarious self. He waved and stepped into line. There were maybe a few hundred of them, awaiting entry to a world of blood and violence.

The chutes were staffed by armed bulls—junior cadets who would one day graduate from Processing to Equality Enhancement and Population Control. Bryan shuffled forward, watching the bulls fingerprint the nervous men. Hand-picked by the Authority, most weren't much older than him. He wondered what would have happened if he'd been tagged for service, all those years before.

Would he have had the stomach to work for the Authority?

"Better not to think of it," a man said in the next line over. He was mousy and slight, with a long, thin nose, wavy black hair and sleepy eyes.

Bryan stared at him. "What do you mean?"

"When that siren went off, a couple of hundred deserters bit the dust. There will be a lot of clean-up in the city today. I saw it in your eyes. You were lost there for a minute."

Bryan nodded. He'd forgotten about the microchips. The bulls were de-activating the Promise Sensors. At least there was *that*.

He pictured the aftermath—the crumpled bodies in city parks, littered along the Oregon Coast, in mountain retreats. Many men simply walked away—content to let the Promise Sensors finish the task without ever testing themselves against the gauntlet of Labor.

"You doing ok?" the mousy fellow asked.

"I guess," Bryan replied. He extended his hand. "I'm Bryan Norton. I live…I live out in Sellwood."

"Fausto," the man replied. "Fausto Ruiz. Goose Hollow. I've got a beautiful little girl waiting on me." The man with the sleepy eyes grinned and it was a relief, like the blink of a lighthouse on the open ocean, to see a positive emotion in the midst of all that naked fear.

Bryan smiled, the thought suddenly occurring to him that there *was* a reward on the other side. Maggie and his little boy. If he could make it through Labor, he'd have a life with his family.

"Nice to meet you, Fausto. You, uh..." He fumbled for the words, and Fausto's grin widened an inch.

"No. I haven't made any connections yet. But I got a good feeling about you, kid. We can work together," he replied.

Bryan felt a surge of relief. There were other rules—rules beyond the three he'd discussed with his pop. Partner up—safety in numbers—was one of them. Look for help on the inside was another one. Something told him the slight man was solid—an ally.

They shuffled forward, maybe a dozen turns until their own. "A little girl, huh? We're having a boy. We'll call him Eli. He'll be here in just a few weeks."

"That's a good name—a strong name. We're calling our girl Carmen. She's amazing! Shoot, all those somersaults in her mother's belly?" he said, grinning at the thought of it. "We're going to have a ballet dancer. She'll be here before we know it."

As they advanced, they swapped details of their lives before pregnancy. When it was their turn, they stepped into the booths.

"Left hand," the bull grunted, roughly seizing Bryan's fingers and running them over the scanner. There was anger in the man's glare, his chiseled features all business. Bryan didn't see so much as a glimmer of compassion in his eyes. The scanner verified his identity. The guard deactivated the Promise Sensor and told him to move into holding.

Fausto waited on the other side and they migrated toward an open space on the perimeter of the holding pen. Bryan craned up on his toes in an attempt to find his father, but his old man had disappeared in the sea of distraught supporters.

"Soooo…right, left or down the gut?" Fausto said when they'd found a quiet place to chat. All around them, men were gathering in loose groups—some big, some small.

"I don't know. You think there have been many changes?"

Fausto shook his head. "I bought a satellite map three days ago. They hadn't raised any forest—least not that I could see. Of course, you know there will be new digital obstacles. Those we'll have to deal with when we get to 'em. But when they open those gates," he shook his head, "this thing is for real. We need to commit to a plan from the start."

Bryan inhaled. "Did the satellite map show anything?" He was jealous of the man's wealth—of his connections. Intelligence on the layout of the Labor field was fiercely prohibited. His father had offered to buy a map, but Bryan had discounted the idea from the start. No sense in committing his family to financial ruin.

"Yeah, I think we position ourselves toward the rear of the crowd. When the lead expires, the bulls will flank us—they almost always do, so we don't want to be in the *very* back. But I think we make a play toward the northwestern quadrant of the field. There's cover there, and lots of different terrain. My information indicates there's an angel in those woods as well. Now, if we can just get to him..."

Bryan made a second appraisal of his new friend. The man might be slight, but he was razor sharp. Despite the sleepy eyes and quick grin, he had a bit of timber wolf in him. Bryan could only guess what kind of man he was outside of all this madness.

"Jesus," he said reverently. "An *angel*."

"That's what my contact said, anyway. We'll see if we can find him. The bulls will try to cut our number in half in that first hour. If we make it to 3:00 p.m., we just might have a chance."

Men were beginning to assemble near the entrance to the field. Fausto and Bryan cut into the crowd and worked toward a position near the back of the throng. The junior cadets had finished processing and were locking down the chutes.

"Welcome," a voice said, booming over the landscape from a pair of speakers on either side of a digital jumbotron, "to the miracle of the birthing process."

A groan rose from the crowd at the sound of the Chancellor's voice. The most vocal supporter of Equality Enhancement and Population Control yet, Adrian Carson was anathema to the men forced to wager their lives for the chance to raise a family. Her severe features—sharp, angular nose and Patrician cheek bones, filled the screen. She had icy blue eyes; Bryan thought he detected a hint of glee in them.

"You have been chosen today to experience the sacrifice and struggle of what it means to become a parent. For the last nine months, your spouse or partner has *devoted herself* to the health and development of *your* child. She has forsaken many of the comforts of our modern existence and endured great physical pain and transition for the singular purpose of bearing *your* child.

"Now, it's your turn to join her on this journey."

Another groan.

"Go fuck yourself!" someone shouted. Bryan watched as one of the bulls raised his head, scanning the crowd for the perpetrator.

"You have my sincere congratulations on making it this far. For twelve months, you've avoided caffeine, alcohol and tobacco. You've gone without comforting medications and you've subjected yourself to the Authority's most realistic equality technology to date—the sleep interval disrupter."

"Jesus. *That* thing," Fausto muttered; Bryan merely nodded in agreement.

"As you are well aware, the world's population has expanded beyond our planet's capacity to sustain a healthy global community. America, in concert with the New Global Initiative, is a foundational participant in the Darwin Culling Process."

Carson paused there in her recorded speech, no doubt aware that the largest protests would follow her statement.

"It is time to return to the principles that made this country great," she continued, that smile expanding on the screen, her perfect canine teeth impossibly white, "*survival of the fittest*. It is time for you to share in the pain *and* the euphoria of a successful Labor process.

"The Darwin Culling Process has met with great success. Our society no longer takes its children for granted. Our culture is no longer scarred by the residual effects of children whose parents have little use for them. Parenthood has taken its rightful place at the forefront of American life. Only the *strongest* may have children. Only the *strongest* survive Labor."

A hush fell over the crowd as the words found their mark. Men turned to regard each other—allies in an ordeal that would mark them for the rest of their lives. Bryan knew the statistics showed that about 5% of those assembled were trying for a second child. The enormity of going through Labor twice was staggering.

"I wish you luck in your journey. The clock began to expire with the noon siren. If you evade Authority forces over the next twenty-four hours, a rich future as a father awaits you."

Carson offered a final serene smile—simultaneously smarmy and patronizing—and then the digital screen went blank. A pair of monstrous metallic thunks shook the ground as the latches sprung on either side of the gate and the great iron wall split in two, the halves slowly sliding aside to grant entry to the Labor field.

"Ok," Fausto said, "stay packed in close here and follow me. If we make it to the woods, we move from tree to tree. Look for something to arm yourself with. I know the bulls patrol for contraband, but you can't keep a tree from tossing a branch. Listen to me," he stared into the boy's eyes, "we'll make it, Bryan."

Norton nodded. For the first time since he'd met the man, Fausto's eyes were wide and alert. The iron gates inched maddeningly across the ground and finally stopped, the red light atop the gateway blinking green.

They had two minutes before the bulls began the slaughter.

The crowd emitted a dim roar as it surged through the open gate and men from all facets of life surged toward the grand ideal of fatherhood. Accountants and mechanics and school teachers and landscapers raced across the open expanse, seeking cover in the distant forest. United by their desire to raise a family, they sprinted into the future.

Bryan and Fausto went with the flow of the crowd, warily trotting into the engineered environment of the great test.

There were five Labor fields in Oregon: Eugene, Salem, Bend, Klamath Falls and Portland. In the middle of the twenty-first century, when the world's population had exceeded eleven billion and the misery of a warm and congested Earth had made life nearly intolerable, the Darwin Initiative had gained traction.

Major American cities cleared space within their borders for immense, wooded Labor fields. In Portland, the field stretched from the banks of the Willamette River up to the university's border and the Park Blocks—eleven square miles of treacherous terrain patrolled by 500 bulls intent on thinning the population.

If it weren't so horrible, the irony would be humorous. The influences of man had inalterably shifted the future of the natural world. Now, man was aiding nature in restoring a balance.

They passed through the gates and onto an apron of compacted dirt. A battalion of a couple hundred bulls, clad in brown military fatigues, their automatic weapons hugged tightly to their chests, stood before a dense forest. The trees were immense, the forest a thick tangle of towering conifers and hardwoods.

Men began to sprint in earnest, Fausto and Bryan among them, for the forest as the clock ticked under a minute. Fifty-eight seconds until the culling.

"There!" Fausto shouted, pointing to the left flank of the bulls. "Pick 'em up, Bryan! It's going to be close!"

300 yards—maybe a little less. Men scattered, a majority sprinting directly through the columns of bulls, trying to disappear into the womb of forest. Fausto selected a spot and began to separate, running in a straight line for his goal.

The man could scoot. Bryan pumped his arms, pulling even as the voice intoned *thirty seconds* over the loud speaker.

They reached the line of soldiers, Bryan glancing into the eyes of the closest. The bull didn't flinch, his gaze trained forward, staring at nothing at all. He was a machine, a simple machine without an ounce of compassion, designed to exterminate those who would dare to compound the Authority's population problem.

To rid the world of another set of lungs—of another mouth to feed, another source of procreation.

"We're close!" Fausto gasped as they reached the first copse of trees. There were paths in the woods, worn routes that snaked through thickets of fern and blackberry brush. A carpet of pine needles and maple leaves crunched beneath their feet.

Twenty seconds.

Bryan thought it was impossible to go any faster, but they found yet another gear. Every second was precious, and in each unit of time was a glimpse at what *could* be. A son or a daughter. A future. A life.

They angled through trees, a smattering of others sprinting through the woods near them, though Bryan sensed that most had chosen the densest portion of the forest, directly beyond that first battery of bulls.

Lungs searing, quads stretched to capacity, Ruiz and Norton strained across the terrain, leaping logs, darting from tree to tree, hurtling brush.

Ten seconds.

"There!" Fausto shouted. Sixty yards away, a gentle hill was peppered with enormous, wispy ferns. There were few trees—few places to take shelter.

Labor…has…begun! echoed the robotic voice, signaling the start of the test. The din of automatic gunfire instantly ripped into the air, a ruckus of destruction and ruin that arced fresh pangs of fear through Bryan Norton's heart.

Fausto hit the hill, began to scramble up it, rolled to the ground and simply vanished.

It happened that fast.

"Fausto!" Bryan shouted, lurching up the bank. A hand shot out from beneath a fern.

"Down, damn it! Move!" the man hissed, and Bryan hit the deck, rolling beneath a canopy of fronds. Fausto was furiously scooping leaves and soil over himself, smearing dirt onto his face, smashing it into his hair.

Bryan followed suit, petrified that they hadn't created enough separation. Here was their first test; they would hide in plain view.

"Quiet now," Fausto whispered, his tone moderating. "We are nothing—nothing more than *mushrooms*, Bryan. We exist in the soil, beneath the protection of these ferns. We are safe, secure down here in the earth."

Streaked with grime, watching the forest from between the shifting slats of gently waving fronds, Bryan felt a stillness welling inside himself. He willed himself down, deep down into the soil, pressing himself into the earth.

They were still.

Periodic gunfire echoed in the forest, but it was dimming, growing faint. Bryan could faintly detect men scampering all around them.

Many minutes passed before he glimpsed the first bulls. In that time, he had learned a few things. Mushrooms are, indeed, *extremely* still.

Mushrooms breathe through every surface of their being, and so did Bryan, feeling himself alive no longer just in the expansion of his lungs, but throughout every region of his body. He drew air through his eyelids, through the backs of his hands, through the skin atop his ankles.

Bryan Norton learned that mushrooms dream, and he fell into his own—dreams not of Maggie and Eli, but of the beauty of the woods, of the green vitality of wild places.

He learned that mushrooms were small, and he too became small.

He learned all of these things as the bulls advanced on the hill. His right eye cracked a centimeter wide, he watched as about a dozen bulls advanced slowly on their position, rifles at the ready. The soldiers picked their way carefully across the terrain, scanning trees for climbers, using the muzzles of their weapons to probe the trunks of enormous rotting trees.

Soon the bulls were beyond ascending the hill; Bryan clamped his eyes shut tight.

Footsteps stippled the ground inches from his face. He felt the tremor in the soil, the way a mushroom would feel the passage of a woodland creature.

The bull passed him, leaves crackling underfoot.

When the sound of their passage grew faint, Bryan sipped the air. He did not move, and neither did Fausto, and in that way the men passed the first seventy-eight minutes of Labor.

"Bryan," Fausto finally whispered. "We need to move. We have three more hours of daylight. If we mean to find our angel, we have to get going."

Bryan took a deep breath. He tried to move his hand to swipe a leaf from his forehead and realized he couldn't move. "I can't..."

"Flex your fingers. Do it gradually. It'll come back to you."

Bryan made a fist, the pads of his fingers exploding in a rush of pin pricks as blood rushed into his hand. He awoke in stages, the agony of disuse powerful in his extremities.

Damn, but life could be hard as a mushroom.

"I'm going to take a look. Wait...don't move," Fausto said. He parted the fronds and glanced into the woods. Slowly, he rose and scanned up the hill.

"Ok," Fausto said, rubbing his biceps and forearms. Bryan joined him and they crouched there, considering their first violent minutes in the throes of Labor.

"Where did you learn that trick?" Bryan asked.

They were hunched, scampering from tree to tree, Fausto looking ahead while Bryan watched their flank.

"I read about it in a book. *The Struggle*. It was written decades ago by one of the Labor pioneers—a fellow named Bic Trenton. He survived *televised* Labor in Miami, back when the Authority was publicly executing dissidents."

Bryan had never heard of the title. Media on surviving Labor was so scarce—the penalty for trafficking it so steep—that the spectacle had managed to sustain its macabre mystery through the long centuries.

They fell into a rhythm, scampering from tree to tree, pausing periodically as fresh gunfire crackled in the distance. They trudged up hills and descended into ravines.

It was in the bottom of one of these ravines that they encountered Derek Gorman.

He sat on a hunk of granite, a look of dazed complacency in his blue eyes, while a cloud of bacteria methodically devoured his left arm. There was nothing left below the elbow and the bacteria were just beginning to digest the flesh of his bicep.

Another batch chewed at the muscle of his right shoulder.

Gorman slowly raised his head at the sound of the men skittering down the steep ravine.

"Oh, shit," Fausto said when he reached the man. "Oh, no."

Gorman offered a weak smile. "Digital obstacle. My advice: don't touch anything."

"What was it?" Fausto asked.

Gorman laughed, the sound a rattle in his chest. "A fucking gun— a prop, of course. I'm so stupid," he replied, shaking his head. "I don't know what I was thinking, you know? I saw it... and I just reached for it without thinking. I slung it over my shoulder. Instant pain."

"And now?" Bryan asked.

Gorman shook his head. "Can't feel a thing. I guess they secrete a chemical or something. Industrious little boogers, ain't they?" He lifted the nub of his arm, a portion of gleaming bone terminating in the ragged meat of his shoulder. "Won't be long now."

Fausto sighed. He bit his lip. "You want...you want me to help?"

Gorman looked at him, a mixture of confusion and gratitude in his eyes. "You'd do that?"

Fausto nodded. "Quick as I can."

Gorman blinked up at the gray sky. He was crying. "What's your name?"

"Fausto Ruiz."

"My name is Derek Gorman. My wife's name is Annabelle. We're having a little girl named Rachel. I want you...I want you to tell them how much I love them. Tell them I'm so sorry that I let them down." His words ended in a little sob. "Tell them I'll wait for them—that I'll be watching over them. Tell them that I love them."

Fausto nodded. "I will, Derek. I will, I promise."

He slipped behind the man and, in one efficient motion, snapped his neck. Gorman's body slumped off the rock and Bryan watched as Ruiz turned and plunged into the creek, fording it quickly and scaling the far banks.

Who *was* this man?

Bryan followed, and they slipped back into their routine. "Biology. Technology," Fausto said. "The Authority has no scruples. They'll take any advantage to execute their policies. We need to do the same. This angel—his name is Fornoy. He will be *our* advantage—*our* equalizer."

"You know his name?" Bryan said. He studied the sky—a thick blanket of gray clouds—and guessed it was after 3:00. They'd made it to their first goal.

Ruiz nodded. "He's a legend. The Authority has been tracking him for almost twenty years. They'd just as soon have him out of the Portland Labor field and be done with him, but he won't go—won't accept amnesty. He's like a shadow—a subterranean ghost. He *believes* in our cause."

"Our cause?"

Ruiz glanced over his shoulder, surprised. "Yeah, our cause. He believes in fatherhood."

Time compressed and the light dimmed. A dull excitement kindled in Bryan's belly. He knew that many had already died— victims of gunfire and, like Derek Gorman, digital obstacles. He estimated they'd covered two or three miles in their methodical fashion. After a time they found themselves on the outskirts of a lush meadow. In the center of the field five bulls, weapons at the ready, surrounded a trio of potential fathers. The prisoners knelt on the ground, hands locked behind their heads.

"Shit," Fausto whispered. He swiped at his brow. "Ok, this is it, Bryan. This is our line in the sand."

"What are talking about?"

"It's just another test," he replied, his sleepy eyes now wide open. "Do we help these men? With our assistance, the numbers are even—five of them and five of us."

"Fausto," Bryan said, incredulous, "those bulls have *guns*. Are you serious?"

"Of course I am," Ruiz replied. "Put yourself in their shoes."

Bryan did. He thought of himself in the center of that meadow and then pictured Maggie; he conjured the images of his father and his mother. He sighed. "Ok, Fausto. I trust you."

While Norton had been lost in thought, Ruiz had scoured their environment. There were things they could use.

Ruiz scampered over to a sizable log. "Here then, Bryan. Lend me your shoulder."

The men hunched at the base of the log. Grunting, they rolled it across the ground, over to a copse of juvenile pine trees. "Ok, we'll need to lever it." He disappeared into the forest, returning a few moments later with a thick bough. "Push. Give it a good shove, now."

Bryan understood what he meant to do and, with the help of the lever and ten minutes of sweaty finagling, they were able to balance the log across the low branches of the pines, just above their heads. The green branches bent beneath the weight of the log, but they held.

Ruiz disappeared again into the forest, returning with a length of blackberry vine. Carefully, he tied the end to one of the branches, drew the line taut and fastened it to an exposed root beneath the trap.

He shrugged out of his windbreaker and delicately draped it over the root.

Norton smiled, shaking his head at the man. "And now?"

"Now we draw their attention." He stooped and began to gather stones. Bryan followed suit. When they each had an armful, they pushed out into the meadow, creeping behind brush as they advanced on the men.

"Where did you get the knife?" one of the bulls asked. Bryan heard the anger in his voice. "Was it Fornoy?"

One of the detainees sniffled, but none of them answered.

"Ok. Have it your way," the bull said. He pulled his sidearm, put it to the head of the sniffler and pulled the trigger, the man's head vanishing in a crimson mist. Bryan saw the men stare at each other in horror. One wet himself.

At that moment, Fausto stood and threw his first stone. It found its mark, cracking a bull on the bridge of his nose with a solid thunk, the soldier's eye socket instantly welling with blood. The bull hunched, holding his shattered nose, and Fausto hurled stones like a pitching machine, rearing back and peppering the bulls.

The captured men hit the deck as one of the bulls sprayed bullets at Norton and Ruiz, the ammunition springing wildly through the air over their heads.

But Fausto was gone, already on the ground, crawling as fast as he could for the tree line. Bryan fanned out wide; he stood and threw his own stones, managing to just take cover as another blast of gunfire ripped through the air above him.

"This way," Fausto shouted, and then they were both angling for the trees. A trio of bulls had pealed away, now striding purposefully for the trees while the guard with the ruined face somehow held the muzzle of his weapon on their terrified quarry.

"Here!" Fausto whispered, and Bryan sprinted for a copse of fallen spruce trees. They pressed themselves against the rotting wood as the bulls entered the forest.

"There," one said, motioning at the windbreaker. "Scan the tag. Let's see who we're dealing with."

Two bulls went to retrieve the jacket. As the shorter of the two picked up the windbreaker, he jostled the vine, tripping the branch and its precarious support of the log. The block of wood lurched and tumbled down onto the men. There was a sound like a cantaloupe falling off a kitchen counter as the shorter guard's skull shattered. The log rolled onto the taller bull, pinning him to the forest floor as a stub of branch pushed deep into his eye, the viscous fluid spilling out onto his cheekbone with an audible popping sound.

"Aw, Christ!" the bull in charge said at the sudden demise of his men; Bryan could hear the confusion in his tone. The bull ducked behind a tree, weapon secured to his chest like a life preserver on the open ocean. "Who's there?" he shouted, his voice high and panicked.

The cries of his fallen comrade were the only reply.

"My eye! Oh God, my eye! Cap, it hurts! Ooohhhhhh, Cap it burns!"

"Calm down!" the bull shouted, voice still wavering. Bryan turned to Fausto for direction but the man had vanished. He understood why when there was a grunt and a sound like kindling breaking. Bryan watched as the captain's body slid out from behind the tree, followed by Fausto Ruiz.

"Come on, Bryan. We've got to do this quickly."

Bryan stepped out. "What do you call that...that trap?"

Fausto picked up the captain's weapon. "It's a Malay Man Catcher," he replied. He handed Bryan the gun and motioned him over to the soldier. "End it."

Bryan took the weapon. He touched it to the man's face, the soldier now quiet, regarding them from his remaining good eye. Bryan heard his father's voice. *You do what you have to, you understand? They'll kill you if they can....*

He pulled the trigger, the man flinching beneath the muzzle, but nothing happened. "Shit," Fausto muttered. "I was afraid of that. Trigger locks."

He took the weapon from the younger man, inverted its stock and rammed the butt of the rifle into the bull's throat, crumpling his trachea. The man gurgled, a look of pain and confusion on his face that morphed quickly into still reservation.

Bryan turned his head, suddenly violently ill. He evacuated stomach bile and water; he was afraid of his companion.

"We need to rescue them," Fausto said. "We can have a chat about morality when this is over, kid."

Bryan wiped away the vomit. He watched Ruiz creep into the meadow, took a deep breath and followed him.

They crept up on the periphery of the bulls. The prisoners whimpered there on the ground—the man who had wet himself had blood seeping from his ear and nose.

Fausto motioned to Bryan, one hand engulfing the other. He held up three fingers. He wasn't sure how he understood the man's directions, but Bryan did. He watched Fausto take a deep breath, steeling himself, and then the man with the tired eyes counted to three.

On three they burst from the brush, covering the space in strides before leaping to take down the bulls. Fausto made quick work of the guard with the ruined face, pulling him into a choke hold before cleanly snapping his neck.

Bryan, on the other hand, wasn't as efficient.

He threw himself into the last bull, hoping to subdue the soldier, but the man had been trained to fight for his life. This man wasn't some abstract rule—he was a living creature, a person with thoughts and beliefs and emotions. Bryan felt him struggling beneath him, the smell of testosterone and fear like burnt plastic on the air, and then the bull freed a hand and jabbed up with stunning force. Bryan was dazed by the blow; he lost his grip.

The bull sensed the shift in control and brought his elbow up into Bryan's temple—once, twice, three times. Bryan felt his strength leaking away; the world went white and then black and he hit the ground.

When he came to, they were back in the woods. "Bryan," Fausto said, his words distant, "Bryan, come on, buddy. Open your eyes."

Norton did. Fausto Ruiz and the two rescued men hovered above him. "We need you to run, Bryan. I know it hurts, but we might only have a minute or two before these woods will be crawling with bulls."

Norton turned his head, straining to process his surroundings. "Ok," he muttered, the pain a spike between his eyes. "Ok—I can...I can do this."

They fetched him up, the men they'd rescued taking a position on either side of him, his arms spread across their shoulders. In that fashion they pushed deeper into the woods.

Soon, they were indeed being pursued. The sounds of the hunt were faint at first, but they steadily grew louder as bulls fired their weapons into trees, ripping apart brush in their quest to avenge the deaths of their brethren.

"Who are you?" one of the rescued men asked Ruiz when they'd stopped to rest on the banks of another creek, their backs pressed against a fallen log. A cold rain was beginning to fall, hundreds of gentle dimples appearing on the surface of the water. Norton thought they maybe had another twenty minutes of light left in the day.

"I'm Fausto. This is Bryan Norton."

"Eric Blaylock," the man replied. The rain had rinsed the blood from his face. He had red hair and fair skin, a grid of freckles over his cheeks and nose and a firm handshake. His sharp green eyes were filled with raw admiration for the man who had rescued them.

"And you?" Fausto said to his partner.

"Bill Boyce. Goddamn, that was really something back there." He shook his head ruefully. "I shouldn't even *be* here. I'm one of the lucky ones—got *two* children at home already. What the hell was I thinking, trying this again?" He was stocky, with thick black hair and large, calloused hands. "Jesus," he repeated.

Fausto whistled appreciatively. "Very impressive, Bill. Are you familiar with this field?"

"Not well enough. I did Labor in Phoenix eight years ago for my first—little Angie. Our boy's name is Ryan. I pulled his Labor here four years ago; honestly, I don't recognize much."

"We're searching for an angel. You know anything about that?"

Boyce shook his head. "Naw. I heard there's a couple in here, though. I thought it was all a bunch of bullshit. Urban legends."

Fausto nodded. "Probably is. Still, we have to hope."

Gunfire popped in the distance, shaking the men from their conversation. They stood, stumbled across the shallow creek and pushed into the woods. After a short time the rain let up and, inexplicably, the clouds parted over the western horizon. The men stopped at the crest of a wooded hill, watching the sun trace its path beyond the ocean.

"It won't be our last," Ruiz said. "Come. We shouldn't stop here. There will be plenty more sunsets for all of us. Come."

The three men started down the hill, but Bryan lingered another moment. Would there be another sunset? Would he and Eli ever have the chance to watch the end of the day together?

It was a shimmering torch, that sun, a beacon of blinding orange light that cast a single tree in silhouette. It was beautiful, and he savored it a moment longer before plunging down the hill in pursuit of his allies.

It didn't take long for the light to fail, and soon they were feeling their way from tree to tree in darkness.

Twenty minutes later they arrived at a small clearing. The smoldering remnants of a campfire lingered at the center of the clearing; Bryan took a step toward it and Fausto jerked him back violently.

"Wait" he hissed.

He found a pine, reached into its lowest boughs and tugged a dying branch free. He packed it back to the clearing and tossed it onto the apron of the fire ring.

A whip-saw twang sounded like a sour note on an old guitar and a thick nylon-mesh net shot out of the loose soil and into the branches of the nearest Sitka Spruce.

The trio of men fixed their gaze on Ruiz. "How in the hell did you know to do that?" Blaylock said.

"It's just caution. It keeps us alive," Ruiz replied. "We've got to move quickly now; I need the three of you to gather tinder. Pick up anything that'll burn. I know they've raked theses woods, but they can't get all of it. This was a mistake on their part. They should have used a digital obstacle instead."

He turned into the woods and began to pick his way through the ferns, searching for dry, organic matter. The others followed suit and before long they had a sizable pile.

Ruiz crept into the clearing, knelt and blew on the dying fire. After a few minutes he'd stoked a honeycomb of red coals on the tip of a small branch back to life. He brought it over to the pile of tinder and got a roaring little fire going.

"Damn that feels good," Boyce said, warming his hands on the edges of the flame.

"Enjoy it another minute. With a little luck, we can use it to put a little more distance between us and the bulls," Ruiz said. He rubbed his hands, crowding the blaze with the damp cuffs of his blue jeans.

He tore one of the sleeves from his shirt and wrapped it around a longer branch. He plunged the tip into the fire, where it quickly ignited.

"That rain we had earlier is no help to us. Still, we have to hope."

Norton appreciated the man's optimism. He'd made the same proclamation a half dozen times since they'd cleared processing.

Fausto strode back into the forest, Eric and Bryan following him. Boyce was trying to light his own torch.

"Under the canopy, things are much drier. Scoop up those pine needles, Bryan."

Norton knelt and began to pile them at the base of a huge group of ferns.

"Good," Fausto nodded, touching the flame to the base of the pine needles. The pile began to smoke and then, with an audible poof, the ferns caught, the fronds curling quickly in the flame. Soon, there were flames licking the lower branches of a couple of the smaller junipers.

Boyce threw his branch into the fray and the men searched frantically for more flammable material to keep the blaze going until the junipers caught. It took some time—time that felt dangerously short to each if them—but soon the junipers were alight and tossing plumes of smoke into the night sky.

Fausto grinned, the expression devilish in the orange light. It completely changed his features, that grin. "Now we run, boys. We run for our salvation. This'll keep them busy for a spell."

He turned and trotted into the darkness. Norton, Boyce and Blaylock, each of them now smiling as well, regarded each other confidently and gave chase.

Though they heard gunfire in the woods, it seemed far behind them. Its repetitive din was now just another facet of the landscape, like the rumble of traffic on the interstate. It was a shock, then, when Chancellor Carson's voice boomed through the woods. It emanated from the trees, surrounding the men.

"Congratulations on successfully navigating your first eight hours of Labor! In sixteen hours, you will be reunited with your family. As many mothers can attest, the deepest hours of the night are often the most uncomfortable. In an effort to ensure a measure of equality, the Authority has taken steps to make your evening in the Labor field difficult."

A bank of lights suddenly slapped on, bathing the woods in a wash of bright yellow light, the men shielding their faces from the intensity of the glow.

In that moment, a platoon of bulls dressed in brown and black camouflage and night-vision goggles rappelled from the towering trees around the quartet. Norton was the first to register their descent.

"Bulls!" he shouted, just as the soldiers opened fire. Fausto tugged him to the ground by his collar, folding him into a roll in the same efficient motion. Norton watched Eric Blaylock's head explode in a film of blood and gore.

Fausto shoved him behind the base of a huge spruce tree and then both men were scrambling into a hunched run, zigging and zagging through as bullets chased them into the woods like shrieking hornets.

An anguished cry echoed through the woods—Bill Boyce. "My leg! Oh god, my leg!"

Ruiz and Norton hurtled a fallen oak, their backs to the skirmish. It didn't seem that the bulls had given chase. Fausto shook his head, distraught, as Boyce's cries escalated. The big man loosed a string of angry insults that terminated abruptly with a single pistol report.

"Shit," Norton whispered, his fear an aching, exposed nerve. Death was close, fifty meters away, and likely once again on the march.

"You hit?" Fausto asked.

Bryan didn't know—hadn't thought to look. "I don't think so."

"Forward then."

They stood and, despite the exposure of the lights (Bryan could now see their stanchions hovering high above the Labor field), they tried to disappear into the woods.

"Murderers!" The bull's call was amplified by a megaphone. "You are both murderers! Ruiz and Norton—we're coming for you!"

"Fuck," Ruiz muttered. He grabbed Norton's sleeve and they began to sprint blindly through the woods, blackberry brambles whipping at their faces as they hopped trees and ferns, barreling toward a future as uncertain as a world with twenty billion souls clinging desperately to its scarred surface.

They ran, hammer flushed down, for almost thirty minutes before Norton couldn't push it any further. "Got to...stop," he panted, strings of saliva trailing from his chin.

"I know," Ruiz agreed. "It doesn't matter anyway. There's just too...too many of them."

Norton looked up, shoulder still heaving, and felt his heart grow cold. The man with the mousy eyes was losing faith. It scared him more than Boyce's shouts or the look of resignation in Derek Gorman's vacant eyes. "We can't...we can't just quit, Fausto."

Bullets cut the air above their heads, tearing into the trunks of hardwoods and pines, blowing splinters into the air like confetti. Branches fell as the gunfire burned a swath through the forest. Fausto raised his hands and slowly turned to face the forest. Norton followed suit.

The lights above them went black and the world was a void—a dense nothing marked only by the bobbing line of red censors affixed to the bulls' night goggles.

"Not bad, you two," one of the bulls called. Norton thought it was the same voice that had echoed through the megaphone. "But it ain't enough, son. You killed good men tonight, you fucking *abortions*."

The venom in the bull's words was palpable. Norton closed his eyes, an image of Maggie the last thing he registered before the world dissolved into chaos and destruction.

He waited for the bullets to rip him apart—bullets that never came—and then the world went utterly silent. When he opened his eyes, Fausto remained at his side. The lights suddenly blinked back on and there were three men behind them, weapons pointed at the ground. Behind them, there was an opening in the dirt with a set of descending stairs.

"This way! Move your asses!" the closest man said. His enormous grey beard had been tied back with rubber bands; the two sections hung from his chin like stalactites. He had wild eyes, thick arms and broad shoulders.

The others disappeared into the earth and Norton peered back into the woods. The bulls lay still in a lake of blood, picked to bits by the gunfire of their rescuers. Fausto clutched his shoulder and then they were on the steps, descending into the earth.

The man with the beard lingered, scanning the forest for witnesses. Satisfied they had not been seen, he followed them, closing the trapdoor behind him, a digital doorway that disguised the fact that any resisting soldiers had ever visited that place in the woods.

"Move," the bearded man said, pushing the awestruck Norton in the back with the butt of his rifle. "Just because you wasted those bulls back at Fornoy's clearing don't mean you're finished with this mess. Pick 'em up, kid."

Norton shuffled forward. They were, remarkably, in a well-built tunnel, the ceiling strung with bare light bulbs. The walkway beneath their feet was corrugated steel, the angles of the tunnel precise.

Jesus. Someone down there had serious resources.

They navigated the corridor and it slowly widened into a hallway, fortified with thick steel beams. Soon there was a pair of double doors and they pushed through them and into a room that hummed with activity. At least a dozen men monitored the struggle taking place above their heads on closed-circuit televisions.

"In here," the bearded man said, angling for an office. Fausto and Norton followed him inside. The man took a seat behind the desk; he rummaged in the bottom drawer until he found a bottle of Pendleton Whisky and a couple of glasses.

"Sit," he said, nodding at the open chairs. He poured three stiff drinks and handed one to Norton and Ruiz. "Hell of a good job so far, men," he said, and they clinked glasses.

Ruiz sipped, Norton eyed his skeptically, and the bearded man tossed his off without another thought. He reloaded and took a sip.

"I'm Alain Verlander. I manage the military ops down here. You, gentlemen, have chosen a hell of a night to have your babies."

"Thanks—thanks for saving us," Fausto said, leaning forward to shake hands with the man. "You work for Fornoy?"

The man shook his head. "Fornoy's dead. Been dead for nine years. Lung cancer. I'm just the next in a long line of soldiers, brother. It's a lineage you'd be right at home in, Fausto. We saw what you did up there. You can handle yourself."

Fausto merely smiled in reply.

"And you," Verlander said, locking eyes with Norton. "You learning anything from your friend here?"

"I...I guess," Bryan said. He shook hands with the man, giving him his name. "I'm just lucky to have met Fausto back there in processing. Dumb luck is what it was."

"Yeah. You could say that," Verlander agreed. Norton couldn't tell if the man liked him or not. He seemed pretty unimpressed.

"You going to drink that?" Verlander asked him, eyebrows raised.

"Oh. Yeah, thanks," Bryan replied. He slugged down half of his drink. It burned his throat and he exploded in a series of ragged coughs.

Verlander and Ruiz chuckled, and Bryan managed a smile when he got himself back under control.

"Come on," Verlander said when they'd finished their drinks. "I'll give you the two-dollar tour."

There was an unobtrusive door behind an immense filing cabinet and Ruiz and Norton followed Verlander into the hall on the other side.

"Infirmary. Cafeteria. Holding cells," Verlander said as they made their way through the network of tunnels.

"I'm sorry," Fausto interrupted, "did you say 'holding cells'?"

Verlander turned and offered them a wide smile. "You want to see?"

"Sure."

A moment later they were in a locked wing. An armed guard sat reading a magazine, on the far side of a pair of double doors. When he saw Verlander, he hastily stood and keyed in the code that unlocked the doors.

"Thanks Jimmy," Verlander said. The guard nodded and then they were in a series of holding cells. There were six of them, packed to excess with naked bulls. It had to be ten degrees colder inside the jail.

Men huddled together for warmth. No one was self-conscious of his nudity—survival was the order of the day.

"Evening ladies," Verlander said. Dozens of hate-filled eyes focused on him. Norton saw a man in the corner of one cell, prone— still. It didn't look like he'd ever move again. "Are we enjoying Labor this evening?"

"Please," came the gasped plea from the back of one of the cells. "Please, Alain. I'm ready to talk."

Verlander scratched his beard in contemplation. He stared into the cell at the haggard man. "Then I might stop back by again in a few minutes then, Skinny. Maybe we'll get you boys some blankets if you're willing to share what you know."

For about the tenth time since noon, Bryan felt ill. He followed Verlander out of the jail, his gaze lingering on the miserable bulls before passing through the double doors.

"What are you hoping to learn?" Fausto said.

Verlander only responded with a Cheshire grin. "In due time, Fausto. In due time. This is operations control. Fornoy laid the foundation for our little resistance here in 2167. Over the last forty-two years, we've been steadily adding to the infrastructure down here."

"And your goal is to...to what? Assist men in Labor? Is that it?"

As he walked, Verlander gesticulated with his hands; he was a charismatic man, a larger-than-life figure. "We do that from time to time. Obviously, we were invested in helping you two out back there." He led them into the cafeteria.

A gaunt man in an apron and chef's hat smiled at them. Quick as a flash he filled three plastic bowls to the brim with white rice and a steaming stew of potatoes and chicken. Verlander thanked him and the men sat, Norton and Ruiz tearing into their dinners with zealous ferocity.

"Careful. You'll burn your mouth. To answer your question, Fausto, we're only partially interested in helping folks along the way. Our primary goal is to topple this here institution. And as providence would have it, the two of you certainly figure in those plans."

Fausto finished his mouthful. "What do you mean? Tonight?"

Verlander shrugged, palms raised. "Here we are. We find ourselves at that strange intersection, boys, between coincidence and fate. The regional general for the Authority is here in Portland this evening. He's overseeing operations. If we can squeeze Skinny in there for a little more information, we'll drill down on his location. We've got a determined group of skilled men, and we'd love to have you both on board. It's pretty clear, Fausto, that you know a thing or two about our struggle." He spooned a bite of stew into his mouth, chewing slowly, allowing time for the words to sink in.

Norton scanned back and forth between the men. He felt a strange confusion in his belly—a mixture of fear and pride. While he remained petrified of dying, he was excited about the prospect of playing a role in what might be an historic event. The emotion surprised him; in his life prior to Labor, he'd never thought of himself as anything close to an idealist. He'd viewed Labor as a necessary evil, a horrible rite of passage that would validate his status as a man and grant him the opportunity to become a father to his child.

But things were changing. He was warming to the idea of striking a blow for men's rights, even if it called for violence. Even if it was nothing more than a symbolic effort.

Fausto, though, appeared conflicted. "I'm not sure I want to take part in what you have planned, Alain. I don't speak for Bryan, and I'm thankful for your help back there—but I didn't come to fight a war. I came to secure my rights to fatherhood."

Alain nodded, chewing his stew with gusto. When he was finished, he pushed his bowl forward on the table and crossed his arms on his chest. "Fair enough. Humor me for a minute, though. If you still want to leave, we'll give you safe passage back into the forest. You can get some rest and see how all of this plays out. And what about you, Bryan? Where do you stand on this?"

"With Fausto," Norton replied without hesitation, drawing a laugh from Verlander.

"Wise answer. What do you say, Fausto?"

"Ok," he replied simply. "Present your case."

They stacked their dirty dishes at the return and followed Alain back to his office. The big man made a call, turning his back and speaking in hushed tones. He poured himself a drink when he was finished.

"This should be interesting," he chuckled. "C'mon. We're headed down to the media room."

The place was packed. The first three rows of seats were filled with heavily shackled bulls in white jumpsuits. They looked grateful for the relative warmth of their new uniforms.

Aside from a few soldiers monitoring the Labor field, the rest of the resistance crowded the seats behind them, making catcalls at the downtrodden men.

Verlander strode to the front of the auditorium. "Ok, ok," he said, "settle down. It's movie night in the underground, boys!"

This brought a roar from the crowd; the bulls looked around nervously.

"Skinny, you ran platoons up there on the Labor field. We know the regional general is in town. We know he's here *tonight*. When you're through watching this, I want to have us a serious talk—see if you can't be a little more cooperative." He motioned to the back of the room. "Roll the film, Trent."

The room went dark and the screen filled with white light.

"Labor," a voice intoned. It was that same animatronic voice that the Authority used in all of its promotional materials. "The experience of a lifetime for dedicated fathers!"

The first image was of an open field littered with the decomposing bodies of men. They covered a huge swath of prairie, the familiar white jackets and sky-blue jeans marking them as hopeful fathers. The ground was like rust with the stains of their blood.

There was a cut to a shot of bulls advancing on a group of fathers, muzzles flashing. The men fell in a heap. A close-up on the smiling lead bull as he lit a cigarette.

The film was about twenty minutes in length—a mixture of carefully edited Authority propaganda juxtaposed with pirated file footage of carnage and chaos on the Labor fields. There was an image of a smiling father holding his recently delivered child juxtaposed with a dead man spread-eagled on the ground, his intestines a slippery coil piled on his midsection.

There were shots of families walking in city parks on sunny days interspersed with footage of headless torsos, victims of promise sensors, likely the result of unplanned pregnancies.

"Labor is flawed public policy," intoned a man near the end of the documentary. He was frail, bearded, propped up in a hospital bed. "It's barbaric. It's antiquated. It doesn't fix our population crisis." He launched into a prolonged coughing fit. "It needs to be stopped."

Fornoy.

Bryan watched the bulls. They were transfixed by the images on the screen. Many of them winced at the visceral shots of the dead. When the film had run its course, the room was deathly silent.

Verlander stood, the white light from the projector casting half of his face in shadow. He looked out at the crowd, his gaze one of unfiltered sadness. There was also an element of anger there. "And who among you is a killer?" he asked softly. "No penalty. Be honest."

The bulls looked at each other nervously. After a tense moment, a single hand went into the air. Soon, every one of them had raised a hand—more than thirty of them.

Verlander shook his head. "God, but it's just such a waste. It's a horrific fucking waste! They train you to kill without conscience. They take away *your* ability to become a *father*. They *use* you. And, in the process, they demean us all."

Some of the bulls nodded their heads slowly.

"We're going to make a statement tonight. If you're willing to stand with us, we'll have you. If not, you're free to leave when this is over, one way or the other.

"Skinny?" He locked eyes with the platoon leader. "Can we have that talk now?"

The bulls turned in their chairs, studying their leader. The man, indeed a rail of a human being, nodded slowly.

"Very good," Verlander said. He freed the man's wrists and they disappeared down the hallway. Soldiers stood and busied themselves with herding the bulls back to their cells.

When it was just the two of them alone in the media room, Ruiz trained his eyes on Norton's.

"Do you want to join them?"

Norton directed his gaze to the ceiling. It took him a long time to reply and, when he did, it was with a simple nod of the head.

Fausto chuckled. "You surprise me, Bryan. And I agree. It'll be dangerous, but we've made it this far. I guess this is our chance."

Bryan nodded. "I think I've sensed that something like this was coming for awhile. I'm…I'm only now opening up to it."

They found their way back to the operations center. Around them, men were laying out kits—weapons, backpacks, helmets. A one-armed soldier chattered into a headset, cataloging the inventory as the room hummed with anticipation.

Forty minutes later, Verlander and Skinny stepped out of the bearded man's office. The room fell silent; Verlander looked at his men, making eye contact with each of them. "We have what we need. Skinny's offered his assistance on this morning's mission. Make your farewells as best as you can; put your affairs in order. We depart at 0100 hours."

There was a moment of perfect silence and then the room swelled with a fresh sense of urgency. Soldiers scrambled back to their barracks, presumably to follow Verlander's advice to make their farewells. The enormity of it all weighed heavily on Norton. He envied them, and he searched for a pen and paper.

Before he could procure them, Verlander was at their side. "I need your decision."

"We'll fight with you," Fausto replied. "This is bigger than any of us."

Verlander clapped their shoulders, his eyes smiling in the fluorescent light. "Thank you," he replied sincerely. "I was hoping we'd have you along. I have a feeling you two play a larger role in this than anyone here can imagine. Is there anything I can do for you in the meantime?"

"I'd like to write a letter," Bryan replied.

"Me too," Fausto said.

Verlander nodded. He left them momentarily and returned with pens, paper and blank envelopes. He pressed them into their hands and left them without another word.

Ruiz and Norton found separate corners of the room, away from the bustle of preparation, and bunkered down to write the story of the war they'd stumbled into.

Bryan felt the writing difficult at first, but soon the words were flooding out of him and he had dappled the pages with a few of his tears as well. When Verlander's booming voice broke the trance of his composition, he'd penned six pages, front and back. "Time to get you outfitted, Bryan."

The thin boy looked up. He cleared his throat. "Ok. I'm just going to finish this...this last thought. I'll be there in a second."

Verlander smiled and Bryan turned back to the page.

> *And so we're leaving soon. I just wanted to say that I love you and little Eli so, Maggie. More than anything in this world. If I don't find my way back to you, please let our boy know that his father died in an effort to make the world a better place for him.*
>
> *Love Always,*
>
> *Bryan*

He folded the note into thirds, sealed it in an envelope and wrote his wife's name on the front. He placed it into the bin with all of the others—the last wishes of a small band of idealists—and went to get fitted for doomsday.

When they were equipped, Verlander stood before them. There were maybe fifty of them in total, including about a dozen of the bulls who had made the choice to fight with them.

"Fatherhood isn't a game. It's not a prize," Verlander began. "It's not a political platform or a social policy. It's not a...not a *carrot* to be dangled over the heads of the people to keep them obedient. It's not a privilege; it's a right. It's *your* right, granted by your biology, *not* by your republic."

Heads began to bob in agreement.

"In these first moments of a brand new day, we will marshal our resources and challenge the Authority. It's been done before. Fornoy stood against them, on this very battlefield, all those decades ago.

There are cells of resistance just like ours, all throughout the country. Throughout the world, for that matter!

"And I'm proud of each of you. So damned proud. Our resolve is absolute. Our will is outstanding. Our mission is righteous. Many of us will die today, but the nobility of our actions will not perish from this Earth."

This brought a roar from the crowd and Norton felt himself swell with pride. He could see the words finding their mark with Fausto as well.

"Skinny believes the bulls are operating out of the old Willamette brewery. It's fortified with four times our number of guards. The general himself will be heavily protected by the Authority's finest. If you get a shot—any shot at all—you take it. If we can topple the regional general, we wound the Authority. This mission is about creating momentum—momentum for others to push for the things that should be ours by right."

Revolution, Bryan thought. They stood on the cusp of a revolution.

Verlander bowed his head and those assembled followed his lead. "God, give us the strength to fight like demons from hell, but with the grace of heaven's angels."

He crossed himself, turned abruptly and strode down the long hallway on the far side of the operations center, flanked by a pair of square-jawed soldiers with red bandannas tied around their biceps. The remainder of the soldiers fell into line behind them and, just like that, they were on the move.

They were quickly topside, trotting through the forest, night-vision goggles locked in place. Norton was amazed at their ability to move so quietly, given the size of their company. They stole across the forest floor like wraiths, the world in front of them lit in shades of eerie green. Bryan occasionally saw the phantom outline of bulls in the distance, but Verlander cut quietly through the trees, deftly avoiding the small platoons of trained killers.

They pounded over pine straw and pushed through blackberry brambles. They moved quickly, efficiently, covering territory at a steady clip. After an hour, Verlander stopped the company at the base of a granite bluff. A shallow creek passed by at their feet; they waded it and massed on the far side.

Bryan and Fausto were winded. Men passed canteens back and forth. They tore into energy bars, clustered around their leader, who spoke in hushed tones. "The brewery sits atop the bluff above us. There are digital moats on three sides of the facility; there's a razor fence on the fourth. Our intelligence shows about one hundred soldiers stationed around the perimeter of the place. The authority has stationed hover lights above us. There are stun canopies in the entryways. Our fight happens here. *This* is where we make our stand.

"Gather your strength, men. Pray to your god. Think of your family. Then…then orient yourselves to the task. We fight hard and we strike the head from the body of the snake.

"There," he pointed at a gentle hill. Norton wondered what it had been all those decades before—before the Labor fields had been created. Maybe a golf course fairway? A lawn at a local college?

"That is our route. We move in single file. We stay low—we stay concealed. Stump here has the codes to disable the eastern moat. That'll be our way in."

Stump grinned in the dark, his teeth dual strings of luminescent pearls. Norton didn't like the smile—it was unnerving—but he was thankful the slight man was on his side.

Verlander allowed the men another ten minutes of rest, then they were moving again. Adrenaline coursing through his veins, Bryan fell in behind Fausto at the rear of the line, the muzzle of his weapon angled toward the ground.

Their objective awaited them at the eastern boundary of the brewery, an ivy-strewn building that was slowly melting into the reaches of the forest. Bryan swallowed heavily. His eyes watered.

Before them was a shimmering field of energy. It looked like black water, but he knew it was electric current—a mirage of deadly technology. On the far side of the illusion, at least thirty or forty soldiers milled about campfires. A line of bulls stood, still as topiary, on the edge of the camp, their eyes trained on the forest.

Here it was. Here it all was, Bryan thought. It was the place where his story would be written—one way or the other. The emotion seemed misplaced, he knew, but he felt calm—satisfied that things would be resolved one way or the other very soon.

From the corner of his eye, he saw a cloud of energy moving toward the moat. It was Stump, crouched beneath a night cloak, two soldiers flanking him with weapons at the ready. Brazenly, they made their way to the edge of the digital obstacle, where Stump fell to his knees. He opened his briefcase, plugged a cord into a box in the ground and began to tap the keyboard of his computer.

Bryan watched all of this, breath frozen in his chest. He let it go in a torrent when Fausto lightly tapped his right shoulder. "You'll be fine, Bryan. We'll make it. When that digital obstacle is gone, we run. We do it for our families—for our children."

Norton nodded. "Thank you, Fausto. I…I owe you my life. I'm here because of you."

Fausto smiled in return. "I look forward to meeting Maggie when this is all done. We'll be ok, kid."

Just as he said it, the digital obstacle disappeared, triggering an alarm. Warbling sirens polluted the air with their cries of calamity; Verlander growled the men forward and their forces sprang into action.

Bryan felt a cry bubble from his lungs, and then he was sprinting toward the camp, bullets snapping from the muzzle of his rifle. The powerful spray went wild at first, but he soon controlled it, feeling a sick elation as he watched his ammunition plow into a group of men sitting around a fire.

The bulls shrieked in surprise. Their cries surprised him and made him feel sick—they were the high and perfectly startled cries of ambushed men.

As the bulls returned fire, he became aware of his comrades falling away. All around him they fell, torn asunder by violence. Bullets whipped past him like buzzing hornets. Fausto took a round in the shoulder and fell to the ground with a sharp cry.

Bryan stopped to help, just as a round caught him in the thigh, passing through his leg and punching out the other side of his blue jeans. He shrieked in pain and disbelief, and then there were hands on them both, half-dragging and half-shoving them toward a little dip in the turf. They fell into the hole as a fresh wave of gunfire perforated the air above them.

"Fausto!" Bryan shouted. "Fausto!"

"I'm here! Aw...shit! I'm ok, I'm ok!"

The man who had rescued them, one of the bulls who had chosen to stand with them, angled up and snapped off a volley of gunfire. He put his back to the ground as bullets chewed the terrain above them. "Three doors on the east side of the brewery," he panted. "We go in at the corner. There's more cover there. Can you two keep going?"

Bryan clutched at his leg. The wound seeped blood—thankfully, it wasn't arterial. There was a groove in his flesh. He pressed down on it, agony flaring through him. "I think so."

"I'm good," Fausto said.

"Ok, then stay low. We crawl. Follow my lead."

They did, and they moved like a trio of phantoms across the scarred ground. Bryan tasted dirt; he felt stones and sticks and grime grinding into his belly. Fausto's boot inadvertently slapped his cheek more than once as they struggled toward their goal.

All around them, the battle was losing steam. Bryan thought the surprise of their attack had led to an advantage, but he knew soldiers were converging on them from other parts of the brewery.

The bull, their hero, looked back at them. "I'm going to blow the door. You'll have to fight your way in. His name is General Creen and he's in the basement."

Fausto nodded, his face deathly pale. He'd lost a lot of blood.

"Listen to me. Please. My name was Ryan Butler. The Authority took me when I was eight years old. *Eight years old.* I'm so sorry…" he said, pausing to gather himself, "I'm so sorry for what I've done."

With that he peeled the adhesive strip from the face of the grip charge he'd been holding and threw it toward the fortified door of the brewery. The charge buzzed through the air, drawing shouts of surprise from the guards stationed there. They dove for cover but it was too late; the explosion obliterated concrete and flesh alike, leaving a gaping hole in the side of the facility.

Butler was on his feet before the charge had found its mark. He ducked the burst of debris and, when the smoke had cleared, filled the space with gunfire. Stunned bulls returned fire, cutting the man down, but his bravery had better than evened the odds for Ruiz and Norton, who easily cleaned up the few remaining bulls.

Norton was unnerved by the stillness inside the brewery. The three of them had killed at least ten bulls—maybe more. He scanned to his right as Verlander guided a group of about twenty remaining soldiers through the campground. Verlander fired single shots from his sidearm into injured bulls along the way.

"Unbelievable!" he said, joining them in the brewery. "I knew you two were something special. Let's move, men! The basement!"

Enormous vats stood rusting on the warehouse floor. The Authority occupied offices against the far wall but, if anyone remained inside of those rooms, Norton couldn't see them.

The remaining fighters formed a loose phalanx, Stump and Verlander and Ruiz and Norton in the center. They crept toward the offices. Verlander stopped them; he motioned silently for his company to make their weapons ready.

Then, as if cued from some producer backstage, armor-clad bulls funneled into the distillery, fanning out behind the vats. Fresh rounds of automatic gunfire erupted in the confined space and Norton understood, in that moment of perfect fury, what the end of the world would sound like.

Norton gulped air as the firefight raged all around them, but they were outnumbered and outgunned.

When the smoke cleared, the room fell silent. "Alain Verlander!" called one of the bulls. "The general requests a conference. We guarantee your safety."

"Don't do it, V," Stump warned. "Shit in staggering amounts is what these ones are full of." Bryan thought he could detect the lilt of an accent—Irish, maybe?

"General Creen guarantees my safety?" Verlander replied. "Is he here? Is he here now?"

"The general is close, Verlander. We can take you to him. Show yourself. Your men will be spared."

In that moment, Norton was all but assured that they would all be slaughtered. The bull's words dripped with treachery. Norton bit his lip, suddenly heartsick for his wife and parents.

"Ha!" Verlander shouted. "Ha, ha! You open, weeping, godforsaken *sores*! You stains upon the face of the good goddamned Earth! You abortions of justice and nature!" He spat the words in a guttural snarl.

"Have it your way," the bull replied calmly. "Archers."

The room went still again, and then Verlander was shrieking at his men. "Cover yourselves! Take cover, men—move!"

There was a flurry of activity and Norton felt Fausto's arm on his shoulder, and then they were sprinting toward a storage closet, the air around them filled with a buzzing like a great swarm of locusts.

Norton didn't know the weapon, but it was cruelly efficient. The metallic points tore into the soldiers of the resistance, cutting them into ribbons and spilling their blood on the stained concrete floor. He heard men screaming, their cries terminating with muted thunks as flesh met steel.

Fausto shoved him into the door and Bryan tore it open just as a volley of arrowheads—heat-seekers, he supposed—sliced into Ruiz's midsection. They exited through his stomach and slapped into the wooden door with a sharp twang.

Bryan screamed and pulled Fausto's limp form into the closet. Outside, carnage raged. He could hear Verlander shouting instructions and then there was a furious explosion, the building shaking as if it sat on an awakening fault.

"Oh, Jesus! Fausto…can you hear me?" Bryan knelt at the man's side, applying pressure to his wounds. "Fausto! Fuck! Come on, Fausto!"

Those sleepy eyes opened. He smiled, a thin film of blood coating his teeth. "Is it finished, Bryan?"

Norton wasn't sure. It had grown still outside—particles of dust and grime drifted beneath the closet door.

"Can you…can you walk? We'll go out together, Fausto. We'll get you some help and get you home to your Carmen."

Ruiz's smile widened. "My Carmen? Yes, my Carmen…I think I can make it, Bryan Norton, for my Carmen. Let's…let's walk out together."

Norton pushed the door open, revealing a ruin of steel and concrete. The far wall was gone. The forest loomed behind a curtain of dust.

Norton supported Ruiz with his arm around his shoulder. They picked their way over the bodies of the deceased, around stacks of rubble.

"Over here," Verlander croaked. He knelt near the ruined body of Stump, whose head and chest just peaked out from beneath a pile of concrete. "He did it. Such a hard man, this little one. We called him Stump, but his name was Jonathan. Jonathan Kenney."

"And now what? Now what do we do?" Bryan said, his tone plaintive. He wept as he felt the life leaking from his friend.

Verlander stood. He bled from multiple wounds. Three of the metallic shafts protruded from his thigh, held fast in the solid bone there. When he opened his mouth to speak, blood washed down onto his shirt.

"Now?" he coughed. "Well, now we finish it. Creen's still here—I can feel him. He'll go down with the ship, if it's starting to flag," he gagged, a geyser of blood staining a crimson bib onto his shirt. "Stump sent out a transmission prior to disabling the digital obstacles. The world knows what we have done here. The world will bear witness. All that's left is to finish it."

They picked their way across the floor to the stairwell, moving slowly, their footsteps echoing heavily on the iron grating as they descended into the bowels of the brewery.

There was a dimly lit corridor at the bottom of the stairs. "A bunker...at the end of the hallway," Verlander panted. He was losing steam quickly. Fausto nodded in and out of consciousness.

Norton was confused. How could he do this himself?

He stopped midway down the corridor, propping Ruiz against the wall. "Wait for me, Fausto. I'm going to get you some help."

The man with the sleepy eyes smiled in return. Verlander slumped heavily against the wall, confusion spreading on his features. "What are you..."

"I need you both to wait here, Alain. Wait for me. I'll meet with the general."

Verlander looked exhausted, his hooded eyes and gore-streaked beard telling the story of a man in his final hour. "God be with you then, Norton." He stumbled, caught himself against the wall and slid into a seated position.

Bryan smiled as the wounded men leaned against each other, forming a crux of support in that dark place. He shrugged out of his rifle, opting instead for Verlander's sidearm.

He walked to the end of the hallway. The door before him had a pane of frosted glass—**LABOR** stenciled on the front in black ink.

"General Creen," Norton called, his tone even. "Come on out of there."

There was a moment of silence, then: "So…Norton is it? Come in, come in. You will not be harmed."

Norton considered the situation. He closed his eyes and saw his wife. He saw his father and his mother—pictured the little house he and Maggie shared in the Sellwood district. He saw the ruined bodies of the men who had fought for the rights to raise a family.

His hand went to the doorknob. It was as though he were outside himself—watching himself enter the lion's den.

He was not afraid.

Creen was very old. He looked frail, his face a story of time and hardship. Still, aged or not, sharp eyes peered out from beneath wild, gray eyebrows. He couldn't discern their color, but they were unwavering.

"Please. Sit down," Creen said, motioning to the chair before him.

Norton did, the muzzle of Verlander's sidearm fixed on the general's chest.

"You have nothing to fear from me, Bryan Norton. You can put that gun away. Or you can keep it out. It doesn't matter."

"Do you have children?" Norton asked. He was surprised by the strength in his voice.

Creen smiled. "I do. My daughter is thirty-six years old. She works for the authority. My son is twenty-four. He will face Labor in four months' time."

"Why? Why would you condone this...this barbaric exercise?"

Creen put his palms up, as if to say *what are my choices?* "This is how it's always been, Bryan. How it's always gone."

"That doesn't mean we can't change it, Creen! We're talking about your son's right to have his own family. Don't you see the flaws inherent in this...this *torture?*"

"My son is strong. He will win his family. Just like you, Bryan Norton. You have navigated the contest. You have survived Labor, and your prize is somewhat grander. Do you mind if I show you something?"

Norton nodded and the general touched a button on the arm of his chair. A bank of video monitors blinked on and Norton's mouth fell open at the images they revealed.

"200,000 of them. Maybe more. The Authority has called in the National Guard. I don't think it'll make much of a difference, though. That," he said, pointing a finger at the monitors, "is the beginning of the end of the current way of doing things."

Norton couldn't reconcile what he was seeing. Throngs of civilians marched up and down Portland's streets. There were, indeed, many thousands of them, pressed into the parks and streets of a burning city. The monitors were silent, but a quality of anger seemed to bleed from the images there.

"If you wanted a revolution…" General Creen whispered, his back turned as he watched the monitors, "you got it."

"And you, General? What will happen to you?"

The old man turned and offered a wry smile. "I'll die. It won't be long now." He rummaged in his pocket, pulled out a canister and threw it to Bryan. Cyanide—a centuries-old manner of suicide.

"Why did you do that?"

"I'm a symbol of the old ways. I understand that. The tides have been turning for decades, but what you did tonight sped things up. There's no life for me on the other side of what happened here, Bryan. No place for me in the new world."

"And your crimes, General? What of the things you did in your life?"

He sucked in a draught of air and let it go in a sigh. "Who knows? I did what was asked of me. Did I believe in it? Sometimes. Early on, mostly."

"Would you change it? If you could, would you go back and change it?"

Creen eyed him. "It doesn't matter, son. Fact is, I *can't* change it. We live with our actions. It's what we…" he grimaced, "what we do."

Norton nodded. He stood and turned his back on the old man and left without sparing him another glance.

When he returned to his friends in the hallway, one was dead. The other barely breathed.

Bryan choked back a sob, threw Verlander's weapon away and sprinted for the stairwell and the promise of help above ground.

***

It was one of those summer afternoons in Oregon. The sky was a rich blue, the trees filled with singing birds. The sun warmed the face of the Earth and their families gathered at a picnic table in Forest Park.

An impressive banquet stretched before them—cold cuts and potato salad and fried chicken and fruit and iced tea and chocolate chip cookies. Bryan sat near his mother and father. Across the table, Eli was strapped to Maggie's chest in a sling.

Fausto played with Carmen on a blanket while Angie, his wife, fixed them plates of food.

"A toast," Bryan's father said. He wore a look of sincere pride as he regarded his son. "To Fausto Ruiz and Bryan Norton—a pair of first-rate fathers!"

There was laughter as they touched cups. Bryan's smile lingered as he scanned the park. Families basked in the sunshine, throwing footballs and eating picnics of their own.

The world had changed in the last nine months. The new government was busy re-building cities toppled by struggle. The Authority had managed a weak defense before falling in less than sixty days to a determined populace.

America was changing. The world was changing.

"Oh, hey now, Buster!" Maggie said, blotting her shirt with a napkin. "We have a code red over here, Daddy!" She wore a bemused grimace on her face. There was a wet circle on her t-shirt.

Eli laughed, his toothless mouth wide in a mischievous grin.

Bryan chuckled. He took his son in his arms, kissing his temple before putting him down on the blanket to change his diaper. It was a small thing, but it made his heart swell with happiness.

Here it was. Here it all was, and the warmth of the day was inside him and all about him, creating a connection to his family that was stronger than the tides of the sea.

ABOUT THE AUTHOR

Daniel Powell teaches a variety of writing courses at Florida State College at Jacksonville. He grew up in Oregon and now lives with his wife, Jeanne, and his daughter, Lyla, near Florida's Intracoastal Waterway. His fiction has appeared in *Redstone Science Fiction*, *Leading Edge Magazine*, *Brain Harvest*, *Something Wicked Magazine*, *Well Told Tales*, *Residential Aliens* and *Everyday Weirdness*. There are many more stories to come in 2011/12. Daniel's web journal can be found at www.danielwpowell.blogspot.com.

For information on Daniel's longer works of fiction, please contact Bernadette Baker-Baughman, of Baker's Mark Literary Agency, at bbaker@bakersmark.com.

www.ingramcontent.com/pod-product-compliance
Lightning Source LLC
Chambersburg PA
CBHW071214130626
46555CB00004B/1700